When Kitty Met the Ghost

Other Titles by Austin Mardon

International Law and Space Rescue Systems
Kensington Stone and Other Essays
Alone Against the Revolution
Political Networks in Alberta 1905-1992

Other Titles by Ernest Mardon

The Founding Faculty of the University of Lethbridge
Place Names of Southern Alberta
Who's Who in Federal Politics from Alberta Ridings
Community Names of Alberta

Collaborative Works by Austin & Ernest Mardon

Alberta Judicial Biographical Dictionary
Alberta Ethnic Mormon Politicians
Alberta Ethnic German Politicians
Alberta Mormon Politicians
Edmonton Political Biography
Alberta Political Biographical Dictionary
Alberta Executive Council 1905-1990
United Farmers of Alberta
Alberta Catholic Politicians
Alberta Anglican Politicians
What's in a Name?
Edmonton Members of the Legislature
Edmonton Municipal Politicians
Alberta Francophone Politicians

When Kitty Met the Ghost

Austin Albert Mardon
&
Ernest George Mardon

Edited by Pauline Balogun
Illustrated by Alexa Guse

Golden Meteorite Press
Edmonton, 2012

Additional Copies can be ordered from:

Golden Meteorite
126 Kingsway Garden
Post Office Box 34181,
Edmonton, Alberta, CANADA.
T5G 3G4

Canadian Cataloguing in Publication data:

Mardon, Ernest G., 1928-
When Kitty met the ghost / Ernest George Mardon & Austin Albert
Mardon ; edited by Pauline Balogun.

ISBN 978-1-897472-37-8

I. Mardon, Austin A. (Austin Albert) II. Balogun, Pauline Jessica,
1994- III. Title.

PS8576.A6463W44 2011   C813'.54   C2011-905774-3

Table of Contents

Kitty & Arthur Conway

The jolly, old town of O'Neill

Chapter **One**

"WELL, HERE WE ARE IN THE JOLLY, OLD TOWN OF O'NEILL in the heart of my highlands and the old land of your mother, my dear," Arthur Conway said, the self-made millionaire and owner of the great Conway Field in Northwest Canada. As he said it, he looked at the other person in the small car.

"Oh, it is lovely, Daddy, darling. It's ever so quiet and peaceful," answered his daughter, Kitty Conway.

Arthur laughed as he climbed out of the car and said, "It will not be so for long. As soon as my little girl gets anywhere, it ends up getting to be quite lively. But, I agree with you that it is quiet for now, in fact, a bit too quiet. And I for one say that it will rain before nightfall."

It was about two in the afternoon when they arrived at the hotel. An elderly gentleman stood to one side, staring dourly at the sky.

"Ay, it will be raining long before nightfall. It always does when new people come by way of Torphin Castle. That there used to belong to 'Be back' Gordon, the Devil of the Dee," the man said in a cracked voice.

"Oh, did you say 'Gordon?'" Mr. Conway asked in a hurried tone.

And Kitty, looking at her father, saw that he had gone quite pale and wondered why. Before the bearded, old man could answer, a cheery voice called from inside the hotel, in front of which the car had stopped.

"Come on, if you want any lunch, you'd best hurry. They are clearing the tables."

The speaker was a cheery-looking man of about forty, who seemed very pleased with himself. As soon as the old man heard the voice from behind them, he started to walk off quickly, after giving Kitty a quick look with his dark eyes.

"Stop!" Arthur cried, and would have followed but for the other man, who ran out of the hotel and quickly put his hand on Mr. Conway's shoulder.

"I would not follow that man, if I were you," he said.

"Why ever not?" Arthur cried, going red in the face, obviously uncomfortable with being treated in this way.

"Because, my dear sir, he is a madman."

"If I wish to speak to a man you call mad, I can and I will," said Arthur in a calmer voice.

"I am very sorry indeed, sir, to interfere with your business. I'll be more careful in the future." The man turned and walked in the opposite direction than the old man had.

"Well, Kitty, that was unusual. Let us go in and see if we can get anything to eat. I do not know about you, but I am simply dying for want of food."

Kitty said, "Oh, let's. I feel so famished I could faint," but she gave her father a peculiar look. It was not like him to get so cross over a trivial thing, but, of course, he had been working far too hard lately. Some strange business had taken up all of his time and a holiday was in order. What a holiday it would be in the Highlands, where Kitty's dear departed mother had spent her childhood. Kitty looked with wonder at the mountain they had just driven through but a short time ago.

"Come along, dear, and don't dally," said Arthur as he disappeared inside the hotel.

But she stood and looked at the mountain and as she looked, a dark black cloud quickly appeared from nowhere it seemed. A cold wind came down from the mountains and although it had been light a minute prior, the land was now cast into frightening darkness. Kitty turned and moved into the hotel and found her father in the hall talking with a man with a grating voice. He looked like a servant and Kitty assumed that he was.

Kitty heard her father say to the man, "Ring White Hall 1212 for me, at once. When you get through, call me."

The man went pale and said, "I hope that nothing is wrong, sir?"

"Why, should there be?" Mr. Conway answered as he held the dining-room door open for his daughter to pass through. The man who was left in the hall looked at the back of the millionaire with fear, but after the door of the dining room closed, he turned and went into a nearby office to make the phone call. When the phone connected, he did not ask for White Hall 1212, but for an Aberdeen number and said in a quick, breathless voice, "Is that you? George Scott –"

"Stop!" The voice on the other end of the wire commanded.

"Why do always call me that name, you fool?"

"I'm sorry, sir. I forgot."

It is your job not to forget. The name is Martin, John Martin."

"Yes, sir, I will remember, sir. You said to send to you the coat you left behind by post, sir."

"Good of you to remember."

"Thank you, sir. The name was John Martin, was it? You can trust me, sir. If there's anything more that I can do, I will, of course. Good-day, sir." The man with the grating voice put down the receiver and turned to face Mr. Arthur Conway, who was standing behind him, hands in his coat pocket and a rather hard smile on his good-looking face.

He spoke in a cold, hard voice that made the man in front of him quickly glance at Arthur's pocket and did not seem happier at the funny little bulge present.

"Ha, I think that we have met before, Mr. Macgregor."

"We met before? Oh no, sir! I have not seen you. I have not, before today, had the pleasure of your acquaintance. I am sorry…" But he never finished what he would have said, for the phone bell started to ring just behind him.

He picked up the receiver and said very hurriedly, "Happy Rest Hotel, O'Neill. This is acting manager Macgregor speaking. Hello, Mr. Martin. You want me to look for a ring in your room…? You say you slept in Number Thirteen. Yes, yes, sir. Good-night, I mean, good-day, sir. Yes, Number Thirteen, good-day." He put the receiver down as if it had become red hot and turned to say, in an oily voice, "And you, sir, want Scotland Yard?"

"And you, most likely, are wanted by the same. In fact, I

have a good mind to give you over to the police here and now."

"No, I would not, if I were you, Mr. Conway. But here is the phone," he turned his back on the millionaire and picked up, for the third time in the last few minutes, the receiver.

Arthur stared at Macgregor intently, in case he tried to pull any funny business, but he didn't notice Macgregor's foot rise. The first thing he knew was that something had hit him very hard in the gut; his gun went off with a bang and by the time he had his balance again, Macgregor was out the door, across the hall and out the front doors.

When Arthur, with Kitty on his heels and the rest of the servants behind her, made outside, the millionaire's car was disappearing down the road in a cloud of dust, the acting manager of the Happy Rest Hotel at the wheel.

Two

"GOOD AFTERNOON, MR. CHARLES DEVONPORT, AND HOW DO YOU feel this sunny afternoon? I hope all is well, even though Mr. Conway and the beautiful Miss Conway are away?"

Charles laughed and replied, "I have been in Kent doing some hard work in a line of very difficult work."

"Oh, Charles, do not tell me," Paul Trent said with mock horror, "that you have, at long last, started to work hard because I bet good money that it would never happen. You, working? Oh, no! It must be a lie. You would surely die, if you did. A dainty fellow like you must only look at the pretty flowers," Paul said with a wink.

Charles rolled his eyes at the implication, but didn't reply. It would stop soon enough.

"What has become of dear, old Arthur? He must be mad, yes, mad, to let this poor, little boy work."

"Stop!" Charles cried, laughing. He continued even while

saying, "I will not let you call me lazy. I always work. Well, I do more than half the time."

"Yet you look like a pig."

"Ah, but I am not a pig. I am only a little fat, just enough to be jolly."

"Well, it really makes very little difference how much, but we all know that you spend the whole day in an armchair, doing nothing at all."

"Oh, stop. You're making me blush. I am getting tired out."

"But, in earnest now, what were you doing in Kent and where are Arthur and the delightful Golden Beauty?"

"In Scotland," came the reply.

"Work or play?"

"Work," Charles replied, "and that is why I am here. Arthur is in Scotland as I said and he wants you brought up to speed on everything, just in case something happens while we're there. I'll be heading there by car as soon as you're caught up here."

Before Charles could start, the phone rang. Trent picked up.

"This is Paul Trent of New Scotland Yard speaking."

The voice from the other end of the wire said, "Just the man I wanted," and continued to talk in a quiet, quick manner. It was, of course, Arthur Conway.

"Is that you, Paul?"

"Yes, sir."

"Well, I want you to tell Charles something for me."

"There is no need. Mr. Devonport is in my office at this very moment. You can tell him directly."

"Oh, if you would not mind, I would like to speak with him."

Paul turned to Charles, handed him the phone and said, "He wants you."

"Right-o," answered Charles as he took the receiver from his friend.

"Yes, sir. Devonport here. What can I do for you, sir?"

"I want you to come to Scotland, at once, and join Katherine and myself. I have something big; by the way, did you find old Mr. Bancanon in that Kentish village?"

"No," Charles answered, "but I have got hold of a picture of the old bird and he does look a little gone upstairs, if you get my meaning, sir."

"Yes, but so have a lot of other good men. More's the pity. Well, you bring Paul Trent up, if he'll come. By the time he gets here something will, most likely, have happened for good or ill."

"And should I tell him our little story on the way?"

"Yes, do that. By the way, dear George Stateman and his friends are around here, so we may disappear all of a sudden. Start as soon as you can, Charles, and go to Torphin Castle, if we are not at the Happy Rest Hotel, in O'Neill. Have a good journey and come quickly."

Charles put down the receiver and turned to Paul, asked him if he was doing anything of any importance and, if not, would he mind coming on a little trip to Scotland where they would meet a millionaire and his daughter. Needless to say, Paul agreed to tag along.

Before ten minutes had passed, they were in Charles' little

yellow racing car and heading north at good speed. On the way, Charles told his story.

He told Paul about Peggy Conway, who, before she had married Arthur Conway, had been the younger sister of the Laird of Torphin, who lived in Torphin Castle. The lands were named after her brother, Roger Gordon. It was six years after she had married and since died, while in Canada. The lands and the castle had gone to her cousin, John Bateing, who still owned it.

Arthur had made money and had come back to England with his daughter. He had made inquiries and found out that the land and castle still belonged to Katherine as the next heir. However, the all-important papers that proved Peggy was the daughter of the old Laird and Roger's sister had disappeared. No one had been able to find them.

Arthur, with Charles' help, had been trying to find someone who had known Peggy well; the resemblance between Kitty and her mother was uncanny, even in their expressions and demeanour. At last, they had found out that Mr. Bancanon had been the gardener when Peggy was a child and that he was hiring in a small village in Kent. But when Charles had gone there, the man had disappeared, leaving behind only a photograph. If Arthur proved that his daughter was the missing heiress, Bateing would have to give up his claim to the estate. Until then, he could stay in the castle and do what he liked with the money. It was said that he was selling the priceless pictures and furniture, so that if it was proved that Kitty Conway really owned the castle lands and the village of Torphin, he could hit the continent with all the money.

It took some time to explain of this to Paul, but at the end he gave a whistle and said, "It's high time you called me. If what Arthur told you over the telephone is true, that this George Stateman or whatever he likes to call himself is around, there is

17

bound to be shady business in the area. That man always seems to be mixed up in rather lowdown jobs."

"If you're around, he might not start throwing lead around like he has in the past," Charles said as he drove along the now dark road.

"What I cannot see is what George Stateman will get out of it." "Ah, there is always a lot to win or lose, if he is in the game, but if we're patient, we will see," laughed the little man from New Scotland Yard. He wasn't laughing at five o'clock the next morning in O'Neill when they found out that the police had been hunting the entire night for one Mr. Arthur Conway and for his daughter, who had gone for a walk during the evening and had not returned.

When Paul Trent heard this, he whistled the tune of 'My Bonnie Lies Over the Ocean' and turned to Charles.

"This is good since we now get to look for them; you can do the work and I can do the thinking." Paul knew in his heart of hearts that it wasn't good. In fact, it probably couldn't get worse.

Three

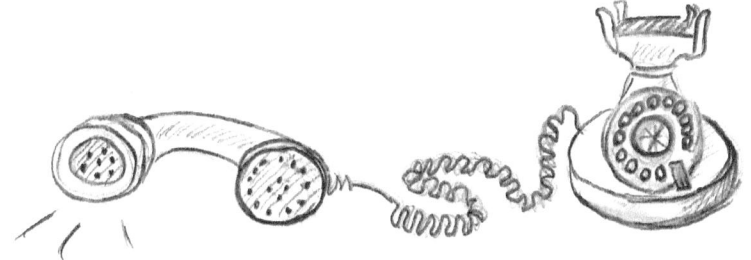

WHEN MR. GEORGE STATEMAN HEARD MR. MACGREGOR TALKING about a ring left behind at the hotel, he thought that one of them had gone mad. It wasn't until heard the word 'thirteen' that he guessed that something had gone wrong, so he waited in the little dark room of the boarding house turned office. He knew that as soon as the danger passed, Macgregor would get in touch with him and the sooner he did, the better.

In fact, as time dragged on, he got more and more displeased and when his phone rang, he had the receiver in his hand like lightning and cried, "Is that you? Macgregor, what is wrong?" Tell me quickly!"

But the cheery answer came over the wire, "No, I'm not Mr. Macgregor. I am John Bateing, calling on business."

"What do you think you are doing, letting Arthur Conway and his girl arrive at the very doorstep of Torphin Castle?"

"Conway is up there! No, he cannot be because he is in Ireland, I am sure – I AM SURE."

John broke in with the same voice, but it seemed harder. "I saw them a minute ago, going into the Happy Rest Hotel where that man of yours is and I hope he has not done anything stupid. He has, I think, or he would have called me. He probably started to act funny. I suppose that Arthur Conway knows, by this time, that something fishy is going on and has come up to see what it is. You should have done as I said and gone south to London to keep them talking down there while my men and I cleaned up this little job. No, I would not let you now because for all I know you might run off with all the money."

"Well, let's not fight and just try to get Conway and his daughter out of the way so we can do as we like. I suppose that I should come out to the castle and help you make plans for getting him and the girl off. So, till we meet again: good-bye." After putting down the receiver, George turned to the door.

Before he reached it, it flew open with a bang and there in the doorway stood Mr. Macgregor with a wild light in his eyes. He cried out in alarm, "The police are after me!"

"What? What do you mean, you fool!?" George exclaimed in a frightened voice. "Don't shout or it is all over for you and for us. Now, speak slowly or I shall give you up to the police."

In about a quarter of an hour, Macgregor had gotten out all the most important things that had transpired at the hotel.

When George understood that even now, the police might be looking for the stolen car, he caught the still talking Macgregor and hurried him out of the house and into the car. He drove off and was soon out of Aberdeen and on the lonely road to O'Neill. About an hour later, he neared the village and turned off the main road and travelled the by-ways to reach the old castle of Torphin, about two miles from O'Neill, but just before he reached the battlements of the castle, he passed through the old village of Torphin, which had been destroyed by fire after it had gone out of the Gordon family and had never been rebuilt by Bateing.

As they waited outside the castle for the gate to open, the sky, which had been overcast for most of the afternoon opened up and in a minute. The muddy road turned into a river. There came a clap of thunder as the car rolled through the water onto the closed courtyard and as the car came to a stop, John Bateing came hurrying across the courtyard. He caught George's hand in an iron grip – he was, of course, the man who had come out of the hotel as Mr. Conway was talking to the old man with the beard.

Bateing said in his cheery voice, "Do come in and get warm. You too, Macgregor. I would like to know how Arthur discovered that something was fishy and why you did not try to bluff him. And you say you had never left the place since you were a child."

"Macgregor could not do that because Mr. Conway had met him before and he would now be in a police station but for the fact that he escaped in Mr. Conway's own car." George said with a slight smile. "But seeing the car here would be too obvious. I think it should be taken apart and moved into the cellars, just in case the police come and demand to have a look at the place."

"Yes, that is a good plan." Bateing took a whistle from his pocket and blew. In a moment, four foreigners appeared and Bateing told them to take apart the car and put it in the cellar.

He turned to George and said, "Now to think of a plan that will get the Conways to leave the highlands."

"It will be very hard," George said with a knowing tone as they disappeared through one of the castle's doors.

21

Four

After Mr. Macgregor disappeared from sight, Mr. Arthur Conway, the millionaire, turned back to his daughter and the hotel staff and said in a quiet voice, "And now I think we have time for lunch, my dear."

"But sir," said the footboy, "the acting manager took your car. Should you not get the police on him as quickly as you can, so he will not get too far? Should I call them, sir?"

"No," Arthur answered, "I do not want the police involved in this affair and the car was an old one anyway. What I do want is something to eat; I suppose it is too late for luncheon now, so what about an early afternoon tea? It's only...what is the time?"

"The time, sir, is just after three o'clock," the footboy said.

All the servants went to their assigned duties and Kitty and her father went into the lounge to be served a genuine Scottish high tea. At the end of it, Arthur Conway leaned back in his chair, lighted a cigarette and said, "I shall step out to use the telephone. Pour the coffee, my dear, while I'm out." He got up and left the room.

Kitty did not pour the coffee, knowing her father and his telephone calls all too well. To her surprise, her father was back in no time at all.

He said, laughingly, "What, you have not yet poured the coffee? You must have been daydreaming again. I'd wager good money that I know who it is!"

"No, you are wrong, for once," Kitty laughed as she poured for two. "I was thinking about your telephone call and whom you were calling."

"Oh, well. As a matter-of-fact, I was telephoning Charles, so I was not too far off, was I?"

"No," answered his daughter as she added sugar to the cups and said, "but what was he doing in Kent? Looking for a house for you to buy or something else? Oh, Daddy, darling, you have been terribly secretive about this whole business. Do tell me all about it now. Come on, you must!"

"Now, Kitty dear," her father said in a kind voice as he took his cup of coffee from her, "sometimes it is better not to know a thing, but if you really truly want to know, I shall, of course, not keep it from you."

"Oh, don't if you do not want to now since I know you will tell your little girl everything, for you always do, in the end," and she kissed her father lovingly.

Arthur said, as he handed back his cup for a refill, "On second thought, I think I shall tell you everything so we can work together. Two heads are always better than one, or so they say. If you promise to be a good girl and do what your dear, old dad tells you, he will tell you a story."

At her nod, Arthur said, "Right, here goes."

And in his good, deep voice, Arthur Conway started to tell his story and no sound was heard in that room save for his voice until the pitter-patter of rain on the roof drifted in. It was soon dark, and still, he went on. The only light was the dying fire, but neither made any move to stroke it. Arthur might have gone on the whole night but for a servant coming in and announcing supper. The servant then turned on the light near the door and it suddenly flooded the room, nearly blinding the occupants.

As the servant told the cook afterwards, both the young lady and the gentleman had been crying about something.

Arthur and Kitty ate supper in silence. Not a word was spoken until it was finished. As they left the dining room, Mr. Conway said to his daughter, "Should we go for a walk, my dear?"

"Oh, yes, it would be quite lovely to see the moon rising up over such an exquisite mountain range. Come on, Daddy," Kitty said.

"There will be no moon tonight," Mr. John Bateing interrupted with one of his best smiles, "but if you would like to go for a drive in my car, I am at your disposal."

"But we are not at yours, sir," the millionaire said in a dry voice, "and I do not wish for you to know my daughter! So if you would let us pass, we would thank you. You must have overheard that we were going for a walk, not a drive in some stranger's car."

"But we are not strangers, Mr. Conway! I was just about to introduce myself. My dear girl, I am your cousin, Sir John Bateing, the present lord of Torphin Castle and the village of Torphin."

Conway then retorted, "And my enemy, if you wish it, so I

would have you make way. My daughter and I wish to go on our walk."

John responded, "All right, have it your way, but you will live to regret it. I, John…"

But that was as far as he got for Mr. Conway leapt to the door of the cellar and swung it open into Mr. Bateing. But before he and Kitty could escape, a servant came out the kitchen to see what was wrong.

"Poor Sir John seems to be having a bad coughing fit and I was just patting him on the back. I think he caught a cold with all this rain. He seems to stand out of doors a great deal; is it any wonder that he's gotten sick?"

"I-I was never outside, Mr. Conway and you do not need to –"

"Oh, you poor man."

Arthur turned to the servant and said, "I think that he has a fever. I think you had better call for one of the castle cars to come pick him up, so he will not get wet on the way back."

"Right you are, sir. I shall do it at once, and see that he's comfortable until the car arrives. I shall see that he gets back safe and sound, sir." The servant bowed and gestured down the hall. "Right this way, sir."

And a furious Laird of Torphin was led away.

"So that is my cousin," Kitty said thoughtfully. "I wonder why he wanted us to go for a drive with him."

"Some fishy business as usual, no doubt!" Her father said. As they were speaking the servant returned from situating Sir John and asked if they were going out.

Arthur informed the servant that they would be going out,

but they would return in no time at all. He also extended his wishes to Sir John that he would suffer no ill effects from being out in the rain. He asked that the fire in his daughter's room be lighted, so that the room would be nice and warm for when they returned.

With that, father and daughter departed arm in arm into the night. They hurried down the empty streets of O'Neill till at last they entered the fields surrounding the village and continued on to the banks of the river Dee. It was there that the millionaire took out his electric torch and a map, which he studied for a time. He then said, "Well, I believe it is upstream from here."

They started off again until the wood in which they were walking gave way to a clearing where they stopped restlessly, waiting for what, they knew not. At last, Arthur broke the silence and whispered in a low voice, "I shall go first and you must not follow me, no matter what happens. There may be shouting and if there is, you will go back and fetch the police and have them search Torphin Castle. If not, you must wait here very quietly. Do you understand me?"

"Yes, Father," answered the fair-haired girl, "but what is this place before us. It looks like – like some trouble already waits there for us. It frightens me so."

"Yes, it does look rather ghoulish at night, but that is only its appearance, my dear. Beyond this is your rightful home— or part of it at least; this is the village of Torphin and while it has burned and lies here in decay, it will one day be rebuilt. I am only going to look around and see if I can find anything that will prove you are granddaughter to the old Laird. I suspect that the papers we are looking for are hidden nearby, if not here, then in the castle although we will not find them there without the help of the police. I should not like to involve them yet if I can, since one never knows how far a man's reach truly is. They may try

26

to do something awful, I'm sure.

"Well, we cannot stand around and whisper all night. Wish me luck," and with that, Arthur disappeared into the ruins of the village of Torphin, leaving Kitty alone with only her thoughts as company.

But not for long; the millionaire was not gone more than five minutes when Kitty realized that she was not alone. There was someone walking behind her.

The sound got louder and louder until it stopped just behind her. She tried to look back, but couldn't bring herself to. She felt her blood run cold until she wondered if she would faint. Using all that remained of her strength, Kitty turned around and came face to face with the most terrifying thing she had ever seen.

It was about the height and shape of a man, but its similarities only made it all the more horrible, the more wrong. Instead of hair, a crown of flames sat on his head and from his back sprang wings tipped with fire. But it was his voice that made him truly terrible. The rasping syllables that fell from its mouth were unnatural and sounded like the sour notes of a violin, harsh in a way that set Kitty's teeth on edge.

"I am the Laird of Torphin; its master is none other. I am the Devil of the Dee. I command thee: begone! No good shall come of thy presence here."

Kitty did not have to be told twice.

As if a switch had been flipped, her tongue loosened and her body was once more her own. With a terrified scream, she took off in a blind run from the apparition that spoke with the cries of the damned and burned with the flames of hell.

Not caring where she fled, Kitty ran faster and faster until the ground beneath her disappeared and she was falling and the sky above could not be seen. Something in her chest gave way and a scream clawed free of her lips and burst toward the heavens. Shocking cold exploded around her and darkness dimmed her eyes until she knew no more.

Five

Mr. Arthur Conway heard his daughter scream as he left a ruined house. He set out at a dead run in the direction from which it came. By the time he arrived, no one was in sight. Only his daughter's handbag remained on the oily grass.

Panicked, Arthur searched the area for some other hint of what had befallen his daughter, but there was nothing. At last, he started to walked towards the road, hoping that whoever had taken Kitty had left a trail there. When he reached it, he saw a car driving up from O'Neill. He dived into the ditch, hoping that he hadn't been seen. The car slowed and came to a stop beside him and the driver got out. It was none other than Sir John Bateing, carrying a box full of what sounded like broken glass. Arthur watched as Bateing scattered the glass across the road.

"What is he trying to hide?" Arthur said to himself. "If he has Kitty, my best bet will be to find out what is going on and use it as leverage."

As Sir John climbed into the car, Arthur took a chance and

climbed into the trunk, hoping that it wouldn't be searched. He felt the car drive off and after a short while, felt it slow and heard the castle gates opening. He heard them shut with a definitive clank once the car was inside.

"I guess that I won't get to leave until I discover Bateing's secret."

The car stopped again and Arthur felt it rock as Bateing got out. He could hear him speaking to someone. Their words were getting louder and Arthur felt a chill go down his spine when he heard them talking about something in the trunk. He listened fearfully as Bateing started to open trunk.

"Darn thing is stuck again."

Arthur swallowed a sigh of relief. He missed what the other person said.

"Yes, it might have. Get one of the men to open it later, but for now, let us go along and see how many of the…"

The words got fainter and fainter and Arthur strained to hear what was being said.

"…we have got…we must…make sure of it."

The voices stopped and Arthur breathed in the silence. He was alone.

He waited a minute to make sure, then crept out of the trunk and looked around. It was dark and Arthur slowly flicked on his torch. He aimed it into the trunk and noticed something he hadn't when he had been inside. There was a false bottom. Hands trembling, he pulled back the cover, reached in and removed a small box. Upon closer inspection, it appeared to be an old cigar box with a small lock on the front. Arthur didn't want to take the time to try and pick it, so feeling slightly frustrated, he placed it in his pocket.

He then started to explore the garage. It seemed much like other garages, save for two high-powered racecars that looked not only new, but very expensive. It seemed normal except for the papers scattered everywhere and the very large pile of them pushed into a corner. Curious, Arthur moved closer, noticing the flagstones beneath him shift. Looking down, he gave the stones a kick. They shifted even more and Arthur pulled them loose. What he saw surprised him. Beneath the flagstones was chamber full of car parts – car parts that belonged to the exact make and model of his stolen car.

Arthur suddenly remembered where he was and quickly replaced the flagstones and hurried out of the garage into a long corridor. There was light further ahead and Arthur decided to walk towards it. As he grew nearer, he noticed a flight of stairs and decided that it might be better to search from the top down. He clutched his torch close, but didn't turn it on for fear of being seen. The castle was so large that Arthur doubted he would run across anyone, but he didn't want to tempt fate anymore than necessary.

He turned it on briefly upon reaching the landing in order to see which way the corridors went. He then wandered around the castle for some time – how long and for what he searched, he did not know – until at last, he went through all of the upstairs rooms and discovered only family pictures and large amounts of dust on just about everything. He wondered what Sir John Bateing saw in the old place. It was nice, of course, but he did not think Bateing was keeping it for that reason. That had to be something else.

By this time, he had gone through half the rooms on the ground floor. It would look, to a stranger, as if the castle was deserted and that no one had been in it for years.

But as he came quickly along one of the corridors, he heard voices from the other side of a door. He fell to his knees, put his eye to the keyhole, and looked through, in wonder, at the scene beyond— and in a moment the secret was no longer a mystery, but clear as day. Unfortunately, Mr. Arthur Conway did not hear the steps behind him until someone jumped on him from behind crying, "I have caught a spy!"

Six

ARTHUR CONWAY, WITH ONE MIGHTY SPRING SIDEWAYS, GOT OUT from under the man and started to run down the corridor, but his freedom was short for as he ran, he did not notice the shadow of a man until it was too late. Mr. Macgregor, for one of the few times in his life, did the right thing at the right moment – by stepping out into the light to see who was coming along the passageway. But for the rest of his life, he regretted it, for Arthur, not seeing him until it was too late, ran right into him. Macgregor went down like a log and Arthur could not help falling over him. Arthur's head hit the wall with a sickening crack and he blacked out.

He could not have been out cold for more than a minute or so since the first thing he knew was that water was thrown onto his face, and he was being helped to his feet in front of Sir John Bateing and George Stateman.

Stateman spoke first, "So you got into the castle, but I think that is bad for you since no one leaves without my say-so and I do not wish to say anything to you, so I am sorry that you will have to stay for rather a long time."

"Where is my daughter?" Arthur inquired in a tired voice.

"Your daughter? I do not know. *You* should though, being her father."

"You know you kidnapped her. You…you—"

"I did not! When was the last time you saw her?"

All Arthur wanted to know was if his only daughter was safe or not. At once, Sir John, George and three other men went to look for her while Macgregor and another man guarded Arthur. He was taken into the room he had spied on through the keyhole. Inside was the biggest counterfeiting workshop that he had ever seen with a large safe in one corner. He thought, 'No wonder.' There had to be at least two or three million pounds in British and foreign currency. This was why Sir John would not yet sell; it was so he could get as much from this workshop and then he and George Stateman would hit the continent and do as they pleased as long as the money lasted— although Arthur suspected it wouldn't last long.

But he wouldn't be able to stop them. Charles Devonport and Paul Trent could do nothing and, most likely, the whole passageway could be hidden and even if the police searched as hard as they could, they wouldn't discover anything fishy. These thoughts swirled through Arthur's mind until suddenly George Stateman came into the room looking very pale and sent Macgregor out of the room.

He came across the room toward Arthur with slow, measured steps until, at last, he stopped in front of him and said in a truly sad voice, "Conway, it is my unfortunate duty to inform you that your daughter is dead. She fell into the river just below the old village of Torphin. We will most likely find her in the morning.

She was not a strong swimmer and the river was swollen from the rain we had this afternoon…"

"You lie…You must be lying. My daughter, my daughter, Kitty wouldn't…" Arthur started to sob, "You must be lying."

"No, look me in the eye," and Arthur did so before turning away with a moan for there was nothing in George Stateman's face that indicated a lie.

"I am sorry for you, Conway," George said in a broken voice, "I have never killed a woman in my life and never planned to."

"Go away! Leave me alone as I now am and will be for the rest of my life," and Arthur Conway, for one of the only times in his entire life, broke down and wept like a child.

He never knew how he got through that night. All he did know was that George came in and said that the police were searching the castle and if Arthur wouldn't mind being quiet. Arthur did not answer and a quarter of an hour later, George left and Arthur was again alone. Even later, one of the foreigners came in and started about their work. Arthur was taken up into one of the towers where the only source of light was a small window overhead.

He walked up and down the room, taking the cigar box from his pocket and on a whim put it into the mattress. Not long after this, Sir John and Macgregor came into the room.

Sir John said in a cheery voice, "I am sorry about your daughter, but if you do things that you should not, you will always get into trouble."

Arthur did not bother to answer and Sir John continued in a harder voice, "I am sorry, but you will have to be searched as we have lost something of great importance."

Macgregor searched all over Arthur's body, but did not find what he wanted. Then, they both hunted around the whole room and at last, they left the room, locking the door behind them. Arthur was again left alone, daylight arrived, and the sun rose in the cloudy sky until about nine when Arthur was startled out of his stupor by the smell of smoke. He ran to the door and recoiled at the plumes of smoke coming from beneath it. He shouted for help, but no one came. He grabbed the poker from the fireplace and started hitting the door. He managed to get it open, but the staircase was already in flames and he was forced back into the room. It was now a true prison with no way out save death. He knew what would happen if he tried to get down the staircase.

The fire had started from the cigar Sir John had carelessly tossed to the floor after leaving Arthur. In no time, the fire had spread and no one knew that almost three upper floors were on fire and their prisoner was in mortal danger.

Arthur knelt down beside the bed and waited. At least, he thought, I will not have to live without my Kitty. I will soon see both her and my Peggy, at long last.

The flames had devoured half of the room and Arthur knew he would pass out long before the first flames reached him, but they grew nearer and nearer. Soon, they reached the bed and Arthur replaced the cigar box back in his shirt. He turned his face to the window.

"It will not be long now, Kitty."

As he spoke, he imagined he saw her in all her loveliness. She was as beautiful as her mother.

Her hand reached for his, "Daddy! Daddy, wake up!"

Poor child. To think that in a minute, he would never need to sleep and he would escape this too-hot room and go somewhere far more moderate. That was his last though before he faded away.

Seven

THE FIRST THING THAT ARTHUR CONWAY, THE MILLIONAIRE, noticed was that it was nice and cold. When he managed to open his eyes, he stared into the beautiful eyes of his daughter.

"Quick. Some brandy, Lan."

He thought that they were in heaven until she said that. He supposed that it was funny to have brandy as medicine, but people didn't get sick in heaven, so he chalked it up to him still being alive and that his darling Kitty was alive too. The brandy burned as they poured it down his throat. In a minute, he opened his eyes and the world seemed to right itself.

In the meantime, Kitty told him what had happened to her since they had parted ways.

The demon-ghost turned out to be Lan Buchanan, a local lad who was unhappy with the new Laird, and who was trying to scare off Sir John and his men. He didn't know that he had been scaring a girl until Kitty screamed. When she fell into the river, he jumped in after her, saving her and took her to his home, a farm that he was working at.

In the morning, Lan showed her a secret way into the castle where she discovered what was going on and that her father was a prisoner. The passageway led them into the room in which Arthur was held captive, arriving just in time to save him from the fire. They were now in the passageway near the end where it came out in the ruins of Torphin Village.

Arthur reached into his pocket and handed the cigar box to Lan, who then opened it. In it was a key and some pound notes. Together, they made a plan and started to carry it out.

Charles Devonport and Paul Trent were in a fix. They had gone over Torphin Castle (twice!) and, save the fire, nothing had been fishy at all. They did not know what to do. Sir John and his old friend were as helpful as one would expect from two men who said they knew nothing about the whole thing. But Sir John said that Miss Kitty Conway might have fallen into the river and drowned.

It was after eleven when they had finished going through the castle for the third time and Paul said, "Oh! Let's go walk up and down outside the castle. I cannot think in this place with all this smoke still hanging around."

"Yes, we might be on the verge of coming up with something — but about that fire: that seems strange enough. Would Sir John really be so careless with a lit cigar and what were they doing up there anyway?"

"Oh, I don't know. I wonder where Arthur and his girl are?

If only we knew!"

"Oh, looks like we caught a break, Devonport. Something seems to be happening finally." As he spoke, a lorry came up from the road to O'Neill and it stopped just outside the castle gate. There were a few words between the local police superintendent and Sir John before they came over to Charles and Paul. The policeman told them that Sir John wanted to deliver his safe to his bank in Aberdeen and if it was all right with them. They exchanged glances. Paul said to Bateing, "Why do you want to move it?"

"Well, I want to get into the safe, but I am afraid that the old castle will burn down," answered the Laird of Torphin.

"All right, go ahead."

At once, the four foreign gardeners, the cook, Sir John and his friend, John Martin, three police and the superintendent went into the library to fetch the safe. They all started to carry it to the lorry. It was a hard business, but in the end it was in the truck. Sir John told the driver that he would drive it himself. In the end, the lorry started off with the four gardeners, the cook and the driver in the back and Sir John and Martin in the front.

The day was foggy and the Scottish Mist was hurrying over the moors. It was altogether a ghostly sight when out of the burnt-out village of Torphin came a frightening sight. In the middle of the road walked a man in black and crowned with flames with wings like a crow, tipped with fire. He looked like the very devil himself. To his side, stood a man, Charles knew to be Arthur, but his clothes were black with smoke and burned. On the other side of the spectre walked Kitty Conway with her long blonde hair all wet and down about her lovely face.

At the sight of this, Sir John fainted and Martin had to lean over to stop the lorry for going into the river. He and Mr.

Macgregor jumped out and ran into the woods.

While a few officers ran after them, Kitty walked up to the safe and inserted a silver key in the big lock. The safe opened and piles of money cascaded out amongst what appeared to be family heirlooms and old documents.

"Look here!" Arthur exclaimed in surprise, reaching amongst the pile for a folder of crumpled papers. "It's a legal document that proves Kitty's the true heiress!"

Charles and Paul stood in amazement, wondering what exactly they had missed on the drive up.

The End.

Join the Conways in another adventure in:

The Girl Who Could Walk Through Walls

When Kitty and her father, Arthur Conway,
disappear under suspicious circumstances, it is
up to their friends, Paul and Charles, to uncover a
sinister plot before it is too late.

Can Kitty and her father survive long enough
for their friends to find them?

Can Paul and Charles save the Conways when
they find themselves in the middle of the plot?

Read *The Girl Who Could Walk Through Walls*
to find out!

Biography

PROFESSOR ERNEST GEORGE MARDON:

He is an English professor who served in the British Army in the Middle East during the 1950s then became a BUP reporter in Northern Canada, then becoming a Medieval English scholar at Red Deer College where he teaches English.

DR. AUSTIN ALBERT MARDON, A.S.M., M.SC.:

He is a widely recognized explorer and scientist, having explored parts of the Antarctic polar plateau searching for meteorites and afterwards presenting his research at the Johnson Space Center. He has travelled extensively overseas in Europe and the Pacific and participated in a scientific exchange in Moscow in 1991, which was cut short his visit with the Soviet Academy of Sciences due to a case of food poisoning.

Credits & Accomplishments:

<u>AUSTIN ALBERT MARDON:</u>

- Written Over 50 Academic Articles
- USA Congressional Antarctic Service Medal: for scientific work in Antarctica on the NASA Meteorite Recovery Program
- Official Texas State Proclamation #51: 1988, for valour.

Ernest George Mardon:

Former Columnist for The Lethbridge Herald

4000 Authored Newspaper Articles

Books:

"The Conflict Between the Individual and Society."

MacLennan, Glasgow.

"The Narrative Unity of the Curso Mundi"

MacLennan, Glasgow.

"Who's Who in Federal Politics"

University of Lethbridge Press, Alberta.

Community Place-Names in Alberta

University of Lethbridge Press.

25 Academic Articles